# I want to be a
# BASEBALL PLAYER

Katie Franks

**PowerKiDS**
press™

New York

*To Green Monster fans everywhere*

Published in 2007 by The Rosen Publishing Group, Inc.
29 East 21st Street, New York, NY 10010

First Edition

Editor: Jennifer Way
Book Design: Ginny Chu
Photo Research: Sam Cha

Photo Credits: All Photos © Getty Images.

Library of Congress Cataloging-in-Publication Data

Franks, Katie.
  I want to be a baseball star / Katie Franks. — 1st ed.
      p. cm. — (Dream jobs)
  Includes index.
  ISBN-13: 978-1-4042-3622-6 (library binding)
  ISBN-10: 1-4042-3622-8 (library binding)
  1.  Baseball—Juvenile literature.  I. Title.
  GV867.5.F73 2007
  796.357—dc22
                                                  2006019459

Manufactured in the United States of America

# Contents

Ichiro Suzuki plays right field for the Seattle Mariners. He is from Japan.

# Baseball Stars

Baseball is called America's pastime. This is because it is one of the most **popular** sports in the United States. Do you enjoy watching baseball games? Do you have a team or player that you follow? Maybe you play Little League baseball or dream of becoming a **professional** baseball player. This book will show you some of the most popular baseball players and the things they do both on and off the field.

Spring training (above) takes place in late February and early March. The baseball season starts in April.

# Spring Training

To play their best, baseball players need to be at the top of their game. That takes practice. Before baseball season begins, teams go to either Florida or Arizona for spring training. Spring training is made up of practice games, in which teams try out their new players with their other players. That helps the team's **manager** decide how to field the players during the season. Many baseball fans go to watch spring training games.

Pedro Martinez pitches for the New York Mets. He is one of the top pitchers in baseball history. He has many special pitches that trick batters into striking out.

# Pitching

Pitchers are important to a baseball team. Pitchers need to throw the ball fast and with good aim. Pitchers try to keep the other team's batter from hitting the ball. If the batter misses the ball, it is called a strike. The person who pitches at the beginning of the game is called the starting pitcher. The pitchers who follow are called relief pitchers, because they give the starting pitcher a chance to rest.

David Ortiz has hit many home runs. He plays for the Boston Red Sox.

# Home Run!

One of the most **exciting** things that might happen during a baseball game is a home run. A home run is when a batter circles the bases and crosses home plate with neither the batter nor any other teammates who were on base getting tagged out. Players who hit a lot of home runs are often the most popular with fans and the highest paid on the team.

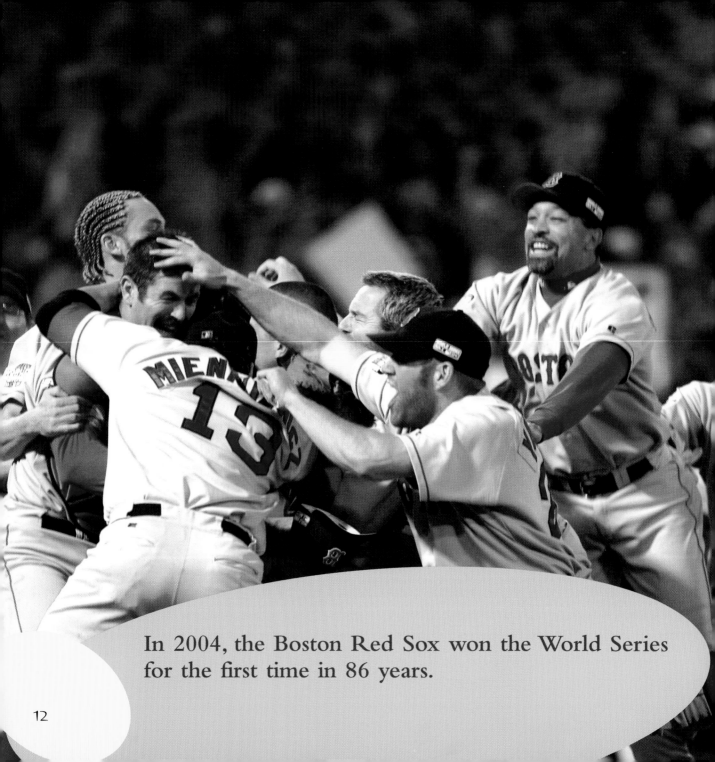

In 2004, the Boston Red Sox won the World Series for the first time in 86 years.

# The World Series

After the baseball season ends, the postseason begins. In the postseason the top teams in each of baseball's two leagues, or groups, play to decide which is the best team in the league. The two leagues are the American League and the National League. The best team from each league faces the other in a set of games called the World Series. The team that wins four of seven games becomes that year's **champion** team.

Albert Pujols plays for the St. Louis Cardinals. He is popular with baseball fans.

# Meeting Fans

Lots of baseball fans would like to have the chance to meet the players they follow. Many fans would also like to get **autographs** if they met those players. It can be fun for the player to meet his fans, too. He can meet face-to-face the fans who clap and shout for him to win games. Players and fans might get to meet after games or at special **events**.

This is Alex Rodriguez of the New York Yankees. Here he is shown working with the Boys and Girls Club in Miami, Florida.

# Charity Work

In their free time, many baseball players do **charity** work. They give their time and money to a cause that is important to them. Sometimes the whole team might work together for a certain charity. Many baseball teams work with the Boys and Girls Club of America. This charity helps poor children across the United States. Doing charity work can make a player feel good because he is doing something for other people.

Derek Jeter is a popular shortstop with the New York Yankees. He has endorsed Ford cars and XM Radio.

# Endorsements

When they are off the field, many baseball stars do **endorsements**. A popular baseball player can make a lot of money endorsing **products**. Companies will pay lots of money for a popular player's endorsement. This is because they know that more people will buy their products if a famous person endorses them. Baseball stars have endorsed products such as Gatorade, American Express, and Nike shoes.

Joe Torre manages the New York Yankees. When he was a player, he played for the St. Louis Cardinals and the New York Mets.

# Managing a Team

When a baseball star **retires**, he may decide to keep working in baseball. One way to do this is to manage a team. A retired baseball player can make a good manager because he has a lot of **experience** to draw on. It is also important for a manager to be able to work well with players. Many retired baseball players have found a second profession in managing.

# The Baseball Hall of Fame

The Baseball Hall of Fame is in Cooperstown, New York. The Hall of Fame honors players who have become baseball **legends**. It is also a place where people can learn about baseball's history. To be **inducted** a player must have played professionally for at least ten years and have been retired for five years. When a baseball star is chosen for the Hall of Fame, he can be proud to be part of baseball history.

# Glossary

**autographs** (AH-toh-grafs)  People's names, written by those people.

**champion** (CHAM-pee-un)  The best, or the winner.

**charity** (CHER-uh-tee)  A group that gives help to the needy.

**endorsements** (en-DOR-sments)  Getting paid to tell people about something they can buy.

**events** (ih-VENTS)  Things that happen, often planned ahead of time.

**exciting** (ik-SY-ting)  Very interesting.

**experience** (ik-SPEER-ee-ents)  Knowledge or skill gained by doing or seeing something.

**inducted** (in-DUKT-ed)  To have made someone a member.

**legends** (LEH-jendz)  People who have been famous and honored for a very long time.

**manager** (MA-nih-jer)  The person who directs a baseball team.

**popular** (PAH-pyuh-lur)  Liked by lots of people.

**products** (PRAH-dukts)  Things that are produced.

**professional** (pruh-FESH-nul)  Someone who is paid for what he or she does.

**retires** (rih-TYRZ)  Decides not to play professionally anymore.

# Index

# Web Sites

Due to the changing nature of Internet links, PowerKids Press has developed an online list of Web sites related to the subject of this book. This site is updated regularly. Please use this link to access the list:
www.powerkidslinks.com/djobs/baseball/